M.V.P.

A PLAYERS GAME NOVELLA

by

RACHEL VAN DYKEN

M.V.P.
A Players Game Novella
by Rachel Van Dyken

Copyright © 2019 RACHEL VAN DYKEN

M.V.P.

DEDICATION

To all of those who have angels in heaven

AUTHOR NOTE

DEAR READER,

This book was originally done in bi-weekly chapters in my newsletter. I compiled the chapters plus two bonus chapters in the end to create this standalone sports romance for everyone to enjoy!

If you finish and want more from this world be sure to check out Fraternize and Infraction. Every book is a stand alone! And don't forget to leave a review even if you hate it! ☺

HUGS RVD

Jax

I WOULD REALLY like to think that in the grand scheme of things, I'm the responsible one, or at least I used to be.

Star quarterback for the Bellevue Bucks, two championship rings in the last two years. Voted People's Nicest Athlete, and all-around good guy.

That was all before.

Before her.

Before I got her pregnant.

Before SIDS.

Before.

All of it was before.

At least that's how I referred to my life back then, it was the before time in my life when nothing could go wrong, when nothing did. Whatever I touched turned to gold.

And now? Now that I'm stuck in the after.

It's all ash.

All of it.

It all started when my dad died. I clung to my fiancé like a lifeline. I held her close. I kissed her belly. I smiled through the tears because we had us, our family.

And then we had nothing.

She couldn't even bear to look at me.

I couldn't bear to look at myself.

I stared down the bottle of Jack then shoved it off the granite countertop relishing the sound of it shattering on the floor.

"Someone's in a mood," came Miller's annoying voice.

How the hell did he end up being the one to clean up my messes? My fuck-ups?

I clenched my teeth.

He was shirtless as he moved his massive body around the kitchen. It had been four weeks since... I couldn't even think about it. I couldn't process it. If I processed it, it had happened.

It couldn't have happened.

Not to us.

Not to us.

I shook my head and stared down at my shaking hands.

"Have you tried talking to her?" He picked up the broken pieces of glass and set them in the sink then came over and pulled out a barstool.

I pressed my lips together.

"Right, so that's a no." He sighed as a light flickered on in the hall. My sister made her way down the hallway, her expression crestfallen as she took in my drunken ass.

"So..." Kinsey flanked my other side, and the sound of the barstool getting pulled across the slate had my ears ringing.

"What are we drinking?"

"You're not drinking," I said in an overprotective voice that sounded fucking scary, like my father had possessed my body and taken over. I wiped my hands down my face.

"Sorry, old habits."

"My wife," Miller said, humor lacing his tone. "Go be a big brother to someone who needs it."

I didn't laugh.

It used to be easy. Sitting with them, laughing, joking. My family, my teammate.

Now I just felt empty.

On the counter, my cell phone buzzed. I scowled and shoved it away.

But when it rang again with the same number, I was ready to throw it against the fridge, was about to when Miller jerked it out of my hand and answered it.

"Hello?" He frowned. "No, he's right here and…" His eyes widened as he jumped to his feet. "What do you mean she doesn't—" He stopped talking, my heart sank, what the hell was happening? "Got it, we'll drive him."

"Drive me?" I tried to stand, but the room started to spin.

"Jax," Miller steadied me, his eyes a bit frenzied. "I need you to listen to me very carefully."

I shoved him away. "I'm not a child."

Just saying child had my stomach rolling. My heart clenching in my chest. "Harley was in an accident, they were doing a photo shoot for that new yoga company, and she fell three stories, broke her leg and—"

"Shit!" We hadn't talked in three weeks. My heart slammed against my chest. When would things get better? When? "

"Jax," Miller's voice softened. "She has a concussion."

"Let's go." I was halfway to the door when his next words slammed into my consciousness.

"She has amnesia. She doesn't remember you."

I fell to my knees, unsure whether I tripped or if my body just collapsed on itself while my heart bled inside my chest.

Arms wrapped around me — my sister.

The love of my life didn't know me. And all I could think was — lucky her.

Why the hell would I ruin the best thing that's ever happened to her?

She doesn't have to remember our dead baby. Or me. She gets a do-over.

I shook my head and whispered. "I'm not going."

2

Jax

1 Year Later
The After

"Your focus is complete shit," Sanchez said under his breath while I threw pass after pass. It was like I'd lost my ability to actually hit my receiver's hands.

"Tell me something I'm not aware of before I ram this football up your ass."

I let out a grunt as I threw again. Sanchez ran his route and caught it, but he had to leap to the right to even make the pass catchable.

I threw off my helmet and kicked it.

Thirty-four years old, and I was acting like a petulant child.

Maybe it was time to retire.

Hang up the cleats.

A familiar ache spread through my chest.

This wasn't the plan.

The plan was to get married to the woman of my dreams.

To fill a brand-new house with children, to wear matching Christmas sweaters and buy a dog.

I leaned over, my hands on my thighs as I exhaled.

"That's how losers rest." Sanchez came up beside me and slapped me on the back just as Miller walked up and basically said the same thing with more profanity.

"I'm just tired." It was utter bullshit; they knew it, I knew it.

They were good friends because they didn't say anything. In all honesty they'd done nothing but be at my side twenty-four seven, giving me updates on Harley and keeping me out of the entire situation as much as possible.

I hadn't just paid her hospital bills.

I paid all her bills.

According to her, she had a trust fund.

Something lodged in my throat; maybe it was my heart trying to make a quick escape and slam itself onto the concrete. I loved her — love her. I swore I'd take care of her forever, I promised my father, her crazy grandmother.

The fact that she didn't remember any of it didn't matter.

I would keep my word.

Besides, things were better this way.

Empty.

Painful.

But better sure.

A few whistles went off. I made my way to the bench and sat. I stared at the turf I'd practiced on since graduating college and getting drafted.

The team I'd led.

Someone sat down next to me. If it was Sanchez, he was losing his head.

I was relieved to glance over and discover it was Miller, who quietly crossed his arms over his broad chest and sighed.

"You should talk to someone."

"I talk to you all the time."

"I don't know how to fix this for you man, I don't know what to do. Kinsey's so worried about you she's losing weight, and you know how I feel about her ass."

I smirked. "Stop talking about my sister's ass before I hand you yours."

"That's the spirit." He gave me a hard shove. "Look, you're going to force her hand, and you know how your sister is. When she gets an idea in her head—"

I squinted as Kinsey started skipping toward us with someone in tow.

"What's in her head?" I seethed.

My heart rammed against my ribcage, rattled it, and shook it like prison bars, like it needed to be set free. A dizzying sensation assaulted me as Harley walked closely behind Kinsey, all smiles.

Her hair was different.

It was longer.

She looked happy, healthy.

She looked better without me.

It hurt to acknowledge that she was the epitome of grace, beauty, perfection, and I was sitting in my own sweat ready to vomit over the loss of her, the loss of our baby.

I couldn't even say the name.

The sex.

It made it too real.

"Your mama misses you so much..." I'd said at the grave yesterday as I put a single red rose on the stone. I read the words engraved through a blur of tears. Three months.

For three months. I'd had the world.

Three fucking months.

"Hey there!" Kinsey said in an alarmingly loud chipper voice that sent me reeling.

Miller stood and pulled her into his arms. "And how's my wife today?"

"Perfect, obviously." She rolled her eyes as he lifted her into his arms and kissed her across the mouth like they weren't in public. He always kissed her that way, like he was contemplating getting her naked every damn time.

And yet we were still friends.

One of life's great mysteries.

Harley's eyes narrowed at me. I waited for it. For her scream of anger and pain. For her tears. For her to tell me she wished she'd never met me. I waited for all of it. I braced for it.

And then she tilted her head and said. "Wait, aren't you Jax Romonov?"

"Yeah," I rasped.

She nodded and then tapped her head. "See? Told you, it's all coming back. My grandma is literally obsessed with you. She says you have the best ass in America. Care to stand and do a little turn?"

It sounded like her.

Every bit.

But if she knew.

If she really knew.

She wouldn't be smiling at me like that.

I had nothing left to offer her but sadness.

I cleared my throat. "Excuse me, ladies." I walked away, surprised when I made it all the way into the locker room before I puked in the first toilet I could find.

3

Harley

H<small>E LOOKED ANGRY</small>.

And then he paled.

And I was left wondering if it was something I'd said or if he was an asshole.

I was going to settle on asshole.

I had the hardest time getting to sleep that night, something about his eyes, his blond hair. Maybe I needed more time to recover, because when I thought of him, my chest hurt.

Why would my chest hurt over a complete stranger?

Maybe because it felt like I knew him?

God knew I had enough Bellevue Buck memorabilia in my house to open up my own sports store. Grandma had said it was a gift from the team.

Just another thing I couldn't remember.

Like what my favorite food was.

I hated that I couldn't remember the little things. I mean,

I knew my name, I knew my social security number for crying out loud.

But I couldn't remember if I'd ever had a favorite color.

I remembered high school.

My first kiss.

The memories came slowly, and I wanted them to get downloaded into my head faster, because then at least I could know how to move on.

It was a weird problem to have. But if you don't know all of your past, how are you supposed to plan your future?

I sighed as my alarm clock went off.

So much for sleep.

I had yoga to teach.

For some reason my friend Kinsey said she thought it would be good during the off season for the guys to do some intense stretching.

And I was the lucky person chosen.

I knew she was just throwing me a bone because of what I'd been through in the past year, but still.

At least it got me out of the house.

It kept me from staring at the stupid football in my room — signed by a jackass who couldn't even make eye contact with me.

"Harley girl?" Grandma knocked on my door then let herself in, she always let herself in, there was zero privacy between us, but we both liked it that way. "Are you headed out soon? I have bacon?"

I grinned. "Well if you have bacon…"

Her smile was wide. "I'm proud of you."

"Thank you." There it was, the shimmer of something in the back of my head, something I should remember, something

I couldn't put my finger on.

"You'll give yourself a headache." She shook her head at me. "These things take time. Now get dressed, get some bacon in that stomach of yours, and do make sure you tell the boys hi."

And that's the other thing. She referenced the Bucks as if she knew each and every one of them personally.

I mean, she knew Miller through my friend Kinsey but she made it sound like she'd spent Christmas with all of them, including Jax.

I gulped as my throat went dry.

Why did he have to be so sexy?

So strong?

I hated that even now my blood heated at the thought of just… touching him.

Yeah, the fall really messed with my head didn't it? Now I want to attack complete strangers just because they smell good and have nice teeth.

I shoved all thoughts of Jax away, hurried to put clothes on, grabbed some bacon, and was out the door in fifteen minutes.

The drive to the stadium didn't take long, and that's the other thing. I knew it by heart, like I'd driven there a million times, and I don't remember ever going to a game.

My thoughts only darkened when I parked in the first available spot I could find. I grabbed my mat and bag from the passenger seat and was just starting to open my door when a sleek Benz SUV pulled up next to me. It was pitch black with tinted windows and dark rims.

Probably another player, one of the married ones who was expecting kids or something.

It was expensive, but for some reason I figured that a

player who had buckets of money would be driving around in a Maybach or something.

I shut the door to my brand-new Jeep and grimaced.

Apparently, I'd bought it before the accident.

But nothing about it was familiar.

It was white with creamy leather.

And it smelled like I'd driven it exactly twice in my lifetime.

I fought back tears of anger at my body's inability to help me out.

And looked up just in time to see Jax Romonov get out of the SUV and glare in my direction.

He clenched his jaw and then shook his head and grabbed a bag from the trunk.

I could handle a lot of things.

But a guy being an asshole just because he has money and a billion women salivating after him just because he could throw a stupid ball?

Pass.

I marched over to him, dropped my bag at my feet, keeping my mat tucked under one arm and said. "Look, I don't know what I did to piss you off, but can we start over? Because I'm going to be busting your ass for the next six weeks on the field, and I can't help you find your inner peace with you shooting daggers at me every chance you get."

"Inner peace." He snorted out a laugh. "Are you actually claiming to already have that?"

The way his eyes twinkled at me stole my breath. He really was bad news, wasn't he? All-American bad boy with too many muscles and a keen intelligence behind his eyes that made me uncomfortable.

"Yes." I found my voice, swallowed, cleared my throat.

"Yoga helps the body and the mind."

He shook his head. "Not mine."

"Excuse me?" I hissed.

"I said…" He towered over me. "…not mine, and it's no offense to you, or to what you're doing for the team. I'm sure all the stretching is going to be great, just stay the fuck out of my head as well as out of my way and we'll be good."

He had the audacity to flash me a megawatt smile that made my brain misfire because for a second I felt like I remembered that smile, I remembered what it felt like to have it directed at me.

But that couldn't be right.

I narrowed my eyes at him.

"See ya later, yoga girl." He grabbed his bag and walked away from me while I stared at him with utter confusion and irritation.

To make matters worse, I couldn't not look at his ass, and I almost punched my own car window when my fingers tingled like they'd actually roamed over that expansive territory he was packing.

No way.

I was hallucinating.

The doctor said that I'd feel confused as my brain tried to unpack a lifetime of memories, and with that, pain. Suffering twice over something you've already atoned for sounded like the worst sort of punishment.

I only hoped that whatever I'd endured these last two years was stupid.

Because in my frail state I wasn't sure I would survive more than a broken fingernail let alone complete devastation over what I was afraid to remember.

4

Jax

IF YOGA WASN'T required by the coaching staff, I wouldn't have stayed. I would have stomped back to my SUV, ripped the door off with my bare hands and… and then what? I wasn't sure.

Anger churned inside my head as my gut swirled with nausea.

It wasn't supposed to be like this.

It wasn't.

"I'll always love you," I'd whispered into thin air that night at the hospital, when she came out of the coma, when she recognized nobody. When the last year was nothing but black dead space. I'd told everyone I wasn't going, and like a coward I'd stood in the shadows with tears in my eyes.

A gift.

It was a fucking gift.

Especially now that the day was getting closer.

I'd need to go to the gravestone. I'd bring flowers for both of us, and I'd continue to mourn what she didn't even miss.

Because she couldn't remember.

I threw my bag against one of the benches then followed the throw with a hard kick, nearly breaking my toe.

"Gotta admit," came Sanchez's annoying voice. "I liked you better before the chip on your shoulder."

"Funny I don't remember giving a fuck." I didn't turn around, just grabbed my water bottle and silenced my phone.

"Maybe you need yoga and anger management," he said in a helpful voice that made me want to throw my water bottle at his face then land a punch to his perfect jaw.

Scowling, I finally turned around. "I don't need anger management. I'm not… angry."

"Nah, you're just heartbroken. When sadness has nowhere to go, it festers and turns into anger. Trust me, you're like one tear away from rotting into a corpse." He grinned. "But never fear, because today, we have yoga!"

"I'm not a corpse." I glared. "And yoga isn't going to help."

"Bullshit, you love yoga or used to. Or maybe it had more to do with a fine piece of ass bending over in front of you?"

I clenched my teeth.

"Joke," he said softly. "Come on, Miller's already out there, they want captains for the first session, then defense, offense, and special teams. The practice squad has a session later tonight."

"That's a long day," I whispered under my breath.

Sanchez flashed me a grin. "Are you worried about her?"

I kept my mouth shut.

"Because if you are—"

"Do you ever shut up?"

"Maybe she would like a sandwich? Some Gatorade? She does yoga so maybe bring her a vegan ice cream." He grinned as we walked into the practice field. "Chocolate."

And he was still talking.

Miller was already with the rest of the captains and co-captains on the far side of the field. And then there was Harley.

In black spandex and a tight purple sports bra with a black crop top falling off the side of her shoulder.

And as I stared.

The anger.

The sadness.

It almost became too much.

I'd gotten her that top.

It was the same day we'd gotten in a fight over money. I wanted her to use my credit cards for everything; she wanted to earn her own way.

But we were going to be married, what was mine was hers.

She said she felt guilty.

So I went to Lululemon and bought one of everything in her size, came home, and told her problem solved. She didn't have to feel guilty because I was the one who did it.

She thanked me with her mouth.

I thanked her back with my tongue.

It was a good night.

It was always good until...

"Just keep your mouth shut," Miller said to me once we got close. "And try not to yell at her for no reason. It's not like she knows."

I grunted.

"You could tell her," Miller offered, his eyes searching mine before shaking his head and looking away. "Right. Let's do this."

With Miller on my left and Sanchez on my right, I didn't really have the opportunity to lash out at Harley.

I did, however, have the opportunity to check out her ass.

And it was just as sexy as I remembered.

As long as she didn't touch me, I'd be fine.

I wouldn't snap.

I wouldn't have a nervous breakdown.

I'd be fine.

"Good," she said a half hour later. "You guys are really flexible, I'm impressed."

"Not as flexible as Jax here," Sanchez piped up. I was killing him later. "He used to date a yoga instructor, so he knows all the moves." And I just moved up that appointment. Killing him now. Right — the hell — now.

"Oh?" Was it me or did Harley look disappointed? Hah, jokes on you because you're the one who taught me everything I know.

"Show me something difficult."

Sanchez cleared his throat while Miller cursed under his breath.

"No, that's okay," I said gruffly. "You're the instructor, I'm just a student. Plus, everyone knows Sanchez is full of shit."

"That's true." Miller laughed along as the rest of the guys started teasing Sanchez.

But the damage was done.

Harley was too damn curious for her own good. "No, now I want to see. Please?" She pressed her palms together. "Tell you what, if you show me a difficult pose and can hold it, then I'll let you guys off the hook early."

"Do it!" The guys started yelling in my direction.

"Fine." I clenched my jaw. *Just don't touch me, just don't touch me.* I moved into a handstand and transferred all of my weight to my right hand spreading my legs. All the guys started cheering at my one-handed tree pose.

I slowly lowered my legs back to the ground and winked at her shocked expression.

"Impressive."

"Thanks." I rubbed my hands on the leggings beneath my shorts and waited for her to say something else.

Instead, she shook her head a bit and then pressed her hands to her temples. I was at her side in seconds. "Are you okay?"

She frowned down at her shaking hands. "No, yes, I think so… I mean you guys are done for the day th-thank you." She pressed her hands together and whispered, "Namaste."

I didn't realize I was still touching her back until she looked up at me with a question in her eyes.

I jerked my hand away. "Are you sure you're okay?"

"No, really, since you're being nice, I must have hit my head or something," she joked, "Not funny yet?"

"No," I said in a strangled voice. It would never be funny. I took a deep breath. "Thanks, Har."

"What did you call me?" she whispered.

I hung my head. Shit. This was why I wasn't supposed to have contact. I mean, among other reasons. Because I knew her, inside and out. We had inside jokes, nicknames, we had habits, and fights. Makeups and breakups. We had a life between us that she didn't know.

And I did.

It was like loving someone who didn't exist anymore.

Like loving a complete stranger who, if they knew the

truth, would hate just as much as you love.

"See ya." I didn't answer her, just walked off.

Hoping she wouldn't chase after me.

And then, stupidly, hoping she would.

5

Harley

"So…" I TWIRLED the straw in my cranberry vodka. "Why did you want to do happy hour here?" I frowned and looked around the hole in the wall bar and grill.

"Oh, you know…" Kinsey's smile was secretive just as Sanchez and Emerson walked up with Jax close behind.

I sighed. "I swear I see him everywhere now."

"Who?" she chirped.

"Your brother," I said through clenched teeth. "I'm assuming he's here because you're here?"

"He was hungry, he's always hungry. I'm sure Miller told him he could come. Besides we used to—" She didn't finish the sentence.

I snapped my fingers in front of her face. "Used to… what? You just stopped talking."

"Harley, if something bad happened but you didn't know it happened, and everyone else did, would you want to know?"

"How bad?" My stomach clenched.

"Bad." She shot me a watery smile. "Bad."

"Would I be missing out on any good?" I asked as everyone approached our table.

Her eyes fell to her brother as she whispered, "Yes."

I followed the direction of her stare and drank in the sight of Jax Romonov like a woman after a juicy hamburger with extra bacon. He had no right to be both pretty and masculine at the same time. And that yoga pose? I was irrationally angry over whatever woman taught him how to do it in the first place. I even had this sudden vision of teaching him myself and laughing as he fell on his face.

Talk about fantasies coming to life!

I needed to chill the hell out before I turned into some psycho stalker who was convinced she's dated one of the league's highest paid quarterbacks.

I frowned. See? Why did I know such useless information? Like he uses Black AmEx cards and flies private?

Why would I have a sudden vision of a jet taking off from the runway, waving goodbye standing outside a town car?

"Helloooooo." Sanchez waved in front of my face. "You feeling better?"

"Yes," I snapped. "Now that you've waved in front of my face, all better!"

He choked on a laugh. "Miss your sass." He grinned and then, "Ouch! Son of a bitch! Who kicked me?"

Emerson shrugged, which meant it had probably been her.

"So..." I looked away from Jax, not that it mattered since I could still feel his body heat from a few feet away. The guy had a presence about him, a magnetism that made me want to lean in even though I knew he was a jerk. "You picked up a stray?"

"Well..." Miller grinned. "I was headed here to join you girls, and Sanchez got his thong in a twist because I didn't invite him, Emerson was waiting outside the stadium, and Jax, well he just looked like a cute lost little puppy. I told him if he shut his mouth he could come, and here we are, all caught up."

Jax snorted.

"See?" Miller laughed. "He's on his best behavior."

"But just in case," Sanchez interjected, "I have a muzzle and leash in my car for situations like this."

"When have you ever had a situation like this?" Emerson wondered out loud, earning an intense stare from her husband.

She turned bright red.

I looked away with wide eyes and heated cheeks.

"So, my appetite's gone," Kinsey joked. "Bring on the drinks!"

I lifted mine into the air. "To being single and ready to mingle."

The table fell deathly silent.

Jax shoved his chair back so hard it hit the table behind us. "I need some air."

With a shaking hand, I put my drink back down. "Did I say something wrong?"

They all looked guilty.

Why did they look guilty?

"I feel like no topic is safe around him," I admitted. "I talk about yoga, he gets pissed. I talk about life, he gets pissed. I breathe air next to him, and he gets pissed."

"Yeah, well..." Miller scratched the back of his head. "It's been a hard year for him too."

"Harder than being hospitalized and not remembering anything?"

"Sometimes…" Miller looked like he was choosing his words carefully. "…it's easier when you forget. Harder when you're faced with it every day like a battle you eventually lose because you need sleep and you can't fight demons for a living. Just… give him time."

"Time," I repeated. "Right." I hopped off my bar stool and made my way outside to where Jax was leaning against the brick building.

"Did you get enough?"

He jerked his head in my direction. "Huh?"

"Air." I crossed my arms and leaned a few feet away from him, mimicking his pose. "You said you needed air after I made a harmless statement about mingling."

"Harmless, yeah," he croaked.

"So, I have an idea." It was a horrible idea, but maybe it would make things better?

"Do you now?" He seemed both amused and irritated.

"Yup." I moved closer. "We should kiss."

His eyes bulged. "Are you seriously hitting on me?"

"No, of course not, I have way better game than that. Give me a little bit of credit," I teased.

He smiled, a real smile.

I liked it so much that I momentarily forgot what I was going to say.

"So," he leaned in closer, "a kiss is going to solve everything, is it?"

"Yeah, I have a theory."

"Well let's have it." His megawatt grin could make a girl forget her own birthday.

"Um…" I lost a bit of nerve as I licked my lips and tried flashing him a confident smile. "It's really easy… we're the only single ones of the group. There's an expectation, but we don't like each other, so we kiss, prove to them and ourselves that it's not going to work out and then we swipe right on someone we really like."

"You wouldn't swipe right for me?"

"Well, now that I know you…" I laughed.

He didn't.

"Kissing me will make things harder, believe me," he whispered cryptically. "I've been told it ruins girls…"

I frowned. "Who would tell you that?"

"A girl." His eyes lit up. "A very beautiful, cunning, sarcastic girl."

"What happened to her?" I whispered, suddenly so jealous of this girl that I was clenching my jaw.

His eyes searched mine. "She hasn't come back to me yet."

"Will she ever?"

"For her sake, I hope not," he said in a sad voice. And then he leaned down and brushed a kiss across my lips, so light, perfect. His tongue moved across the seam of my mouth and then he slid it past the barrier of my lower lip and tasted me, I wrapped my arms around him on instinct.

And I knew what would happen next.

I wasn't sure how I knew, just that I did.

He braced me against the wall, he gripped my hips like he was afraid to let go, and my heart beat in a steady rhythm that pumped heat into every part of my body.

Jax pulled away, his palm cradled my face. "Did it help?"

I shook my head no.

He kissed my forehead and whispered, "Told you so, Har."

And then he was walking away.

And I was staring at him in confusion.

Because that was the second time he'd used a nickname like we were long-lost friends.

Because when I closed my eyes and touched his lips.

I felt strangely like I was home.

6

Jax

FIVE MILES.

A fifth of Jack.

And I was still staring at the TV trying to remember when I'd turned it on and when my life got so pathetic that I was drinking alone, sitting in my own sweat, wondering why the universe was punishing me.

They just had to invite her.

And I just had to kiss her.

I licked my lips — couldn't help myself — she was there.

Damn it, she was everywhere.

In everything.

From the candy she'd hid in the pantry, to the toothbrush I couldn't bring myself to throw away in the master bathroom.

To all of the baby stuff I'd surprised her with still locked away in one of the spare bedrooms.

I knew what I would see when I walked in there… Walls

with yellow paint because she loved yellow.

And memories.

So many horrible memories of her in the hospital sobbing, and me feeling like the most hopeless dick on the planet.

I would have died for her, for them.

Willingly.

Survivor's remorse was real — even when you never truly knew the one who died or got to see them grow up — it still exists, still happens.

And I felt guilty that an innocent life was gone.

And I was still sitting there, breathing air.

A knock sounded on the door.

I ignored it.

The knock got louder.

With a curse, I stood on shaky legs, stumbled a bit, and jerked it open.

"Hey." Harley gave me a weak smile and then held out a brown paper bag. "You took off so fast, your food came, and I drew the short straw so… here you go."

"Nice. I'm the short straw?" I leaned against the doorframe and drank her in, from the full lips I'd just tasted to the slight dimple in her right cheek as she crossed her arms in a protective stance.

"Well you're not exactly a joy to be around." She scrunched up her nose. "I could make you soup or something." She frowned harder. "I have a feeling soup will be the only thing that makes you less grumpy. Hamburgers are gross anyway."

I did a double take. "Did you just say hamburgers are gross?"

"Duh!" She rolled her eyes and shoved past me like she owned the place, which, surprise, surprise — she did. I would never take her name off of what I'd already given to her.

Never.

At least if I died she'd know that she was taken care of. For life.

I wondered if she'd forgive that.

Knowing that she would never get the last word in.

The final goodbye.

"What the hell are you doing?" I shut the door and faced her while she started rummaging through my kitchen. Did she realize the ease at which she did it, like she wasn't a stranger?

Like she was the one who'd organized it in the first place?

She grabbed a pot, opened the fridge and then gripped the handle to the fridge and moved back until she braced herself against the granite counter.

"What?" I tried to sound innocent.

She blinked and then shook her head. "I know this fridge."

"It's a popular fridge." I shrugged then moved toward the bar and pulled out a stool. "It's been on TV, trust me, everyone knows this fridge."

"No, no not like that." She pointed. "I know where everything is."

"Because I'm a neat freak," I lied. Of course she did. Damn it. Why couldn't she just leave it alone? Why couldn't she just leave? And why didn't I have the heart to kick her out?

Probably because seeing her in my apartment, in my place, where I'd been with her for months, made me feel like coming home for the first time since we'd lost the baby.

I squeezed my eyes shut while she jabbered on and on about all the places I kept my vegetables, only to pull out a few things, grab a cutting board, again without hesitation, and a knife.

I relaxed when she started chopping.

And then nearly swallowed my tongue when she pointed the same sharp ass knife at my face and said, "Did we know each other before my accident?"

I grit my teeth and hissed out, "Yes."

"Did we…" She gulped and then her cheeks flushed bright red. "Did we…"

I grinned and stood, towering over her. "Did we… what?"

"Um…" She waved the knife in front of us and then pointed toward the hall. "Did we… date?"

"Hmmm, can't say we ever labeled it like that."

Her eyes widened. "Was I a one-night stand?"

"Never." I shook my head vehemently. "You're not that kinda girl…"

"But we did…" Her eyes searched mine.

I licked my lips and leaned over. Only part of the granite countertop separated our bodies as I tilted my head and whispered, "We did."

She sucked in a breath.

"Often."

"How often?"

"Often enough that I know you have a birthmark on the inside of your right thigh just below your ass cheek." I smiled. "It's ticklish."

The knife clattered to the floor. I rounded the kitchen island and stalked toward her as she moved toward the stove.

Then I cornered her, a hand on each side of her. "And you're loud, really loud. Your grandma almost caught us once."

"Oh how great… for us." She gulped. "So, what happened?"

I hesitated.

She blinked up at me, lips parted, eyes wild like she wanted me to pounce, like she needed it more than anything in this world.

"What do you think happened?" I countered.

"Did you break my heart?" She lowered her head, clasping her hands together like it was already true.

"No," I said softly. "You broke mine."

7

Harley

My hands were shaking at his words.

I broke *his*?

Impossible.

Who left… that?

I turned, locking eyes with him. He was so tense I could see his jaw harden with each second that ticked on in silence.

"I don't believe you," I whispered.

His lips twitched and then he was picking up the knife off the floor, rinsing it off and handing it back to me. "Believe it."

"Is that why you hate me?"

His body tensed even more. "I don't hate you. I could never hate you."

"What happened?" I set the knife back down and crossed my arms. I figured I'd probably slice a finger if I tried to multi-task at that point.

Body rigid, he hung his head and swore. "Thanks for the

hamburger, but I should probably get to bed."

"You go to bed at eight?" I countered.

His lips twitched. "That's my polite way of kicking you out."

"Because I'm making you talk about your feelings?" I was grasping at straws, but what else was I supposed to do? The guy refused to explain anything. Tears stung the backs of my eyes. Would it always be like this? Living in the present with shadows of my past haunting me? "How else are we supposed to be friends if I don't know what happened?"

"Friends." He said the word like he hated it. He scowled and then pressed his lips together like he wanted to reject the word altogether. "I don't think that's ever going to happen, Har."

"That!" I pointed. "Right there."

He tilted his head and crossed his arms. "What?"

"You don't just give someone a nickname when it's casual sex or even just dating for a few weeks, right?"

He looked away, jaw tight. "You really should go."

"What did I call you?" I took a step toward him, knowing he'd probably retreat but for some reason needing comfort even though I knew that was probably the opposite of what was on his mind. "Did I have a nickname for you?"

He licked his full lips. "You mean other than perfect?"

"Hilarious."

"You used to pause the game on my ass and send me screenshots, but you never called me anything other than my name." His eyes looked so sad as they searched mine like he was willing my body to remember something but at the same time hoping it wouldn't.

My cheeks heated. I reached out to touch him but stopped

when he flinched away. "I was wondering..."

"What?" he croaked.

"If I could... maybe since you were part of my past..." I chewed my lower lip. *Well here goes!* "If I could touch you, just for a few minutes, maybe it will help spark some memories of us?"

His eyebrows shot up to his hairline. "You're full of shit, right?"

"No." I got closer. "What if it helps?"

"Exactly." He snarled out the word. "What if it helps and you remember how much you really do hate me. I'll make it easy for you," His teeth clenched as he balled his hands into fists and towered over me. "You told me you never wanted to see me again, you said you hated me, you screamed at me." My body shook as it took each blow.

I almost didn't trust my voice. "What were we fighting over?"

"Does it matter?" He hissed, bracing my shoulders. "You have a life now, you're awake, stop thinking of the past and live in the present."

I wanted to slap him. "Something tells me I'm not the only one living in the past."

His lips parted.

"What? Nothing to say?" I reached out to touch his chest, not really sure why except it felt right.

He squeezed his eyes shut, the heat from his skin was almost burning my fingertips as I ran them down his muscular arms, and then finally gripped his hands in mine, both of them, fingers interlacing.

He tried to pull away.

But I knew he didn't want to. Because he was huge, and if

he didn't want me to be touching him, it wouldn't be hard for him to jerk away and hide behind a potted plant.

"You feel so warm." I leaned closer.

He met me halfway.

And then his hands were in my hair, my waist, his mouth pressing hungry kisses across mine as he lifted me onto the kitchen counter and deepened the kiss like he'd been waiting for years to touch me, maybe his whole life.

I clawed at his shirt and returned the kiss with equal fervor, and all the while the back of my head pulsed like a headache was coming.

He jerked away and did a small circle covering his face with his hands. "You need to go. Now."

"But—"

"Now!" he roared, eyes wild. "I mean it, Harley. This will never happen, not again, you think I'm being cruel and you don't even realize, this is the nicest thing I could possibly do for you. The kindest. The best. This is me loving you like I always will — from far away."

"You love—"

"Go. Now." His voice cracked as he turned on his heel and walked down the hall. I heard a door slam.

My eyes filled with tears as I looked around his beautiful lonely kitchen, and then like my legs had a mind of their own, I walked to one of the cupboards, opened it, and pulled out a bag of candy.

As if I'd put it there.

Frowning, I grabbed a mini Snickers and then shoved the candy back.

Except behind the candy was a Polaroid taped to the wall.

Of me and Jax.

Kissing.
While I showed the camera my diamond ring.

8

Jax

I WASN'T SURE what was worse.

The front door slamming, reminding me of the last time she'd done it, the last time she'd shattered my heart into a billion tiny unrecognizable pieces, or the sound of her soft sobs as she did it.

Was that it, then?

History had nothing better to do with my life than fucking circle around and give me another broken heart? What? It didn't do a bang-up job the first time?

"What the hell do you want from me?" I yelled at the ceiling then buried my face into my hands as I sat on my bed.

Alone.

As I reached for her old pillow, squeezed it between my fingertips and the faint fragrance of her Prada perfume fill the air.

It wasn't fair.

Wasn't this the part of the story where something magical happened? The universe sent someone to make it all right? Or maybe you got a re-do and you were told that you could take one road and live happily ever after?

I wanted that road.

Hell, I'd been on that road.

I was living my happily ever after until the universe ripped us both from the story, cursing the rest of my life.

I threw the pillow against the wall and lay back against the mattress. Time passed, I wasn't sure how much, maybe an hour, maybe two.

I couldn't sleep.

And part of me was afraid that if I did, I'd forget what it had been like to taste her again, to feel her body against mine, to dig my hands into her hair to give those same pieces of hair a tug and moan into her mouth.

My eyes burned with tears I refused to shed, not because I was trying to be tough but because I was so fucking afraid that if I broke — there would be nothing left.

Just an empty shell.

A heart that refused to work.

And a mind that couldn't focus on anything, not even football.

The door to my apartment opened again.

The hell?

I shot up to my feet in time to see Harley tentatively walk into the master, like she'd done a million times before when she had lived with me.

It was too familiar.

It was cruel.

I hated everyone.

Everything.

It wasn't fair.

"Please." My voice cracked. "Go."

"Where is it?" Her eyes were crazed. "I just went back to Grandma's. I looked through everything, I can't find it, I need to find it!"

"Harley?" I took a step toward her. "What's wrong?"

Tears spilled over onto her cheeks, she quickly swept them away and gave me a terrified look. "I woke up feeling naked, you know that? Like I was missing something, like my body was empty but more than that, it was deeper than that, even my hands didn't feel the same and I couldn't figure out how hands could feel different. I mean how does a person's hands just change after a coma?"

My gut twisted. "Harley you aren't making sense."

She stomped toward me and shoved at my chest. "I'm not making sense? We were engaged! Unless that was just a celebratory picture where you were congratulating me on a new boyfriend I must have been cheating on you with! What the hell!"

I missed her spark.

I missed that terrifying feeling in my chest when she raised her voice, when her anger was directed at me,

I missed the feeling because I knew I was the only one in the universe who could make it okay.

She'd said so.

All the time.

My throat clogged. I had nothing to say that she didn't already know. "How'd you find out?"

"I was hungry," she grumbled, crossing her arms as more tears spilled. She seemed angry that she was wasting them, the tears, and I wondered in that moment if it was because she somehow knew deep down inside that she'd spilled too many over us and that it was my turn to pay up. "I remembered a bag of candy." She put up her hand. "Don't ask me how I knew, I just knew that you had a stash. I reached for it, and behind the candy was a Polaroid of us kissing and me with my engagement ring."

"Right." That was all I had? Right?

Her eyebrows shot up. "Anything more you want to add to this conversation?"

"Not really. No." I gave her my back and plopped back onto the mattress at just about the time she started jerking open my drawers and tossing my clothes out onto the floor like she was searching for drugs.

"Harley!"

"What?" A shirt went flying by my face followed by boxers.

"I'm looking for my ring!"

"Why? So you can pawn it?" I roared, jumping to my feet again.

She froze.

I immediately regretted the words, but that was the thing. Once they're said, once the person hears them, they can't really be taken back. Nor can the impact they have on the person you meant to hurt.

"I didn't mean that," I said softly. "Why do you need the ring?"

Her shoulders slumped, and then she collapsed to the floor in a heap of sobs, wrapping her arms around her legs, ducking her head as if she was trying to protect herself.

I reached down and pulled her to her feet, then into my arms. She didn't protest, only proceeded to cry against my shirt harder as I carried her over to the bed. Knives pricked my chest with each step, damn it, damn it, damn it.

I laid her down and then sat down next to her. "Are you going to be okay?"

"Do I look okay!" She threw her arms out, her hair went flying, her cheeks were red and puffy, and her eyes were bloodshot.

I'd never seen anyone so beautiful in my entire life.

I cupped her cheeks, brushing away her tears with my thumbs, wishing I could taste the saltiness and kiss them away like she deserved. "Maybe not right now, but you will be, eventually. You need time."

"No, I need you to be honest with me."

"Maybe I'm too selfish for that." I lay down next to her, my eyes facing the ceiling as I put my hands behind my head and let out a sigh. "Maybe I'd rather have you close and feel your hate, then have you far and not feel anything at all."

"That's the saddest thing I've ever heard," she whispered.

"Life is sad." I swallowed my tears again.

She didn't say anything for a few minutes.

Frowning I looked down at her in time to see her mouth part open as she snuggled against me and put her hand on my chest like she used to.

Just like old times.

Fantastic.

And yet I couldn't bring myself to yell at her or kick her out.

So, I stayed there, in a Hell of my own making, and rubbed her face sending her into a deeper sleep all the while wondering how the hell I would ever live without her.

When I knew keeping her would be the cruelest thing I

would ever do.

9

Harley

I DIDN'T WANT to wake up.

I wanted to close my eyes and imagine a world where I was still in this man's arms, where I didn't have a brain injury, where I didn't feel that loss and emptiness in my soul every single time I stared at myself in the mirror.

I felt like someone had given me a puzzle with only half the picture and pieces that all looked the same.

Nothing fit.

Except one thing.

I fit.

I fit in his arms.

Like God had created this space right next to his body — where I was meant to lay.

My eyes were still closed.

He shifted next to me.

I was suddenly hyperaware of my hands. I had one tucked

under my head. The other was on top of ab number three.

I really liked the feeling of his hard body beneath my palm, the steady breathing and rise and fall as he inhaled, exhaled. I liked the peacefulness of being next to him.

My left leg was thrown over the lower half of his body. If I moved a bit closer, I would be fully straddling the guy.

Butterflies erupted in my stomach as realization kicked in. I had been engaged — not just dating, but engaged to this guy.

This huge massive man.

A guy who had been on the cover of People.

America's quarterback.

He was the next Tom Brady.

And he'd proven it over and over again.

Holy shit! I'd slept with him!

Hadn't I?

Had we been naked?

In this bed?

My body buzzed with awareness as I fought to gather at least one memory of these pillows, of the white duvet I was lying across. But I had nothing except blank space.

I sighed in frustration.

"How long have you been awake?" he rasped, voice all sexy and full of sleep and promises of multiple orgasms via his tongue.

Damn it!

Why couldn't I at least remember the good parts?

"Yeah…" I answered, and before chickening out blurted, "Did we have sex in this bed?"

He was quiet.

And then he gradually moved to a sitting position. My hand fell away from his body as I watched him slowly shake his head and then turn to me, eyes so intense I couldn't look away. "We rarely made it that far."

I felt my own eyes widen. That was his answer? We never made it that far? "Because…" I licked my dry lips. "Because, we were…" I didn't finish my sentence.

His grin was devastating. "Because I'm not patient, and every time it came to you—" He tugged at my shirt, fisting it in his hand like he was going to rip it to shreds.

Dear God, please Edward Scissorhands my shirt and throw me against the mattress like a UFC champ.

"Oh." I waited for him to make the first move.

Instead, he swore, released my shirt and stood, running his hands through his hair like he was frustrated with me. "I should get ready for practice."

"Yeah, you don't want your yoga teacher pissed at you."

"Hah!" He barked out a laugh. "Well I've been on the opposite end of her temper more times than I'd like to admit. I think I know how to handle it."

"Maybe I've changed." I crossed my arms, a bit offended but also not wanting him to get ready, because it meant I had to leave. It meant this moment, whatever it was, would be over, and I needed it. I needed him.

He tilted his head then leaned over, his massive body coming within inches of mine as he put his hands on my shoulders and then very slowly pulled me to my feet.

I exhaled a shaky breath as those same hands ran up and down my arms, only to stop as he crooked my chin with his thumb and forefinger, leaned in and whispered in my ear, his lips grazing my skin, "I highly doubt it."

I was afraid to breathe.

He lingered there like he was seconds away from kissing

my neck.

And I would let him.

My heart pounded in my chest as he slowly pulled away and then gave me his back. "Spare towels in the cupboard. If you want to shower, I'll feed you before you go."

I stared after him, stunned. "Are you going to poison my oatmeal?"

"Bacon," he corrected moving out of the room. "And I'm not going to poison you… yet"

"Why the sudden change of heart?" I called after him.

He stopped and looked over his shoulder. "I'm not as strong as I thought I was."

"It takes strength to stay away from me? I'm not sure if that's a compliment or an insult."

"Oh, I'd take it as a compliment. Now I'm going to leave before I do something we both know we'll regret."

"What's that?"

His eyes locked on mine and then lowered, never had I ever seen such a sexy look on a guy's face before. I squeezed my thighs together as the corner of his mouth tilted up in a smirk that should be illegal. "Use your imagination. I know I am."

I gaped.

"Oh, and you're going to want to brush—" He pointed to my head. "—all of that."

I touched my head. Sure enough, my hair was a mess. I probably looked homeless.

"Brush in the right drawer."

He shut the door quietly behind him.

Disappointed, I stood there for a few brief seconds then opened it a crack and watched him walk down the hall cursing the entire way. And I might have smiled a bit when he adjusted himself and banged his head against the wall at least three times before disappearing around the corner.

Game. On.

10

Jax

I STARED HARD at the bacon, the pan, the utensils. I figured if my focus was elsewhere I'd lose my shit, march into that bathroom, and slam her against the nearest sturdy surface, lick her from head to toe, repeat, and then burst into tears.

Actual tears.

This wasn't how it was supposed to go.

She was supposed to hate me.

She was supposed to stay away.

She wasn't supposed to know where the candy was, or why her finger still had a small imprint from the rock I'd put there.

And that wasn't all of it.

There were so many secrets between us, I could have built a wall to Heaven only to jump back down into Hell the minute she looked at me and realized the truth.

I was keeping the most painful parts of our relationship to myself, holding them with my bloody beaten hands, I was giving her a free pass, and I was going to make her fucking take it, if it was the last thing I did.

The bacon was cooked.

I worked on a few eggs.

I numbly walked around the kitchen and set her plate down in front of one of the bar stools and then grabbed my cell.

She needed closure.

I would give her the only kind I knew how to give.

I dialed the number.

Of course, she picked up on the first ring. "Jax?"

"Yeah, hey, you free tonight? I was thinking dinner?"

"What are you doing?"

"Please?"

"Jax…" She was hesitating. I knew why. We'd been friends forever. But she was beautiful, and she would make Harley second guess, she would help me push her away.

Damn it, why was it so painful?

My chest felt like it had taken so many brutal hits, there was no way my heart wasn't exposed like this giant raw nerve.

"Fine," she said. "I'm assuming you want this front-page news?"

"Please." I choked down the word and waited a few beats before hearing another sigh from her.

"You owe me, Romonov."

"I know, Noel."

"Eight?" She sounded disappointed in me. Then again, she'd known me since I started in the league. She was the GM's daughter, had always been off limits to the team, but after everything with Harley she'd reached out as a friend.

And I'd used her ever since.

To keep up appearances.

To make everyone think I was completely fine.

When I was dying inside.

"Yeah." I hung up.

We'd go to the usual spot.

We'd laugh and eat dinner, we'd put on smiles for everyone. I'd show everyone that I was fine, I'd prove to Harley our chapter was closed, and Noel would prove to the last jackass running back she dated, that she'd moved on to bigger fish.

"Hey!" Harley rounded the corner and then plopped down on the barstool the way she used to.

My mouth went completely dry.

Her dark hair was wet, and she was wearing one of my cotton white shirts that hung past her hips.

Was she even wearing underwear?

I fisted my hands to keep from reaching for her and checking.

"What the hell are you wearing?" I asked in a tone that bordered on murderous.

She grinned. "A shirt. Just like you are. Anyways, I was thinking, after the bacon you have practice, weight lifting, yoga with yours truly."

I suppressed a groan.

"Why don't we hang out after?"

"Not happening." I handed her a fork. "Eat."

"Someone's grumpy this morning." She dug into her eggs with fervor and then shoved a piece of bacon in her mouth. I'd always been obsessed with the way she ate.

A woman who enjoyed food as much as she did was just... a beautiful thing. I never had to worry about some weird diet if anything I was more restricted in what I ate than she was.

"I'm not grumpy, just exhausted, and I have a long day." I stared at her pointedly. "Harley, I know you want answers." She paused mid-bite.

"And the truth is…" I felt like I was going to throw up. "The truth is, I've moved on, and I think you should too."

"What?" Her face paled. "What do you mean you've moved on?"

"Dating," I lied. "I'm in the process of moving on, and I think considering the circumstances, it would be healthy for you to do the same." That sounded good, right? Even though I was minutes away from running in the opposite direction full speed toward a wall to purposely knock myself out.

"What's her name?" She narrowed her eyes and kept eating.

"What?"

"Her name, the girl you've moved on with." She waved the bacon in front of my face and then bit down with a grin. Damn, did she have to be so sexy? I was ready to crawl out of my skin. Torn between biting her and biting into my dry toast.

God, she'd tasted good.

Smooth skin beneath my fingertips.

Smiles against my mouth in between kisses.

"Noel." I crossed my arms. "And the rest is none of your business."

"So, you wouldn't mind…" She didn't miss a beat. "…if I went and just made out with what was that guy's name? The hot wide receiver?"

I grit my teeth. "Which one?"

"You know, the one with the ass." She waved her fork at me and then stood and slowly walked around the island.

I backed away. "They all have asses."

"No, you know, the one that the Sports Illustrated body

issue said was carved from actual stone, Isaac was it?"

Isaac fucking Roberts?

No. HELL. No.

The guy had slept with half of Seattle and Bellevue by now!

"That's not moving on, that's a one-night stand." I gave her a challenging glare. "I mean truly moving past all this shit and finding someone who will make you happy."

"That's the problem, Jax." She had me cornered against my own damn stove. "I'm pretty sure you're the only one who can do that."

"And I'm pretty sure; I'm the only one who's not willing."

She flinched.

I hated it.

The pain I saw in her eyes.

The knowledge I was the cause of so much of it.

"Just leave it, Harley. Leave us."

"We're not worth fighting for, then? Is that what you're telling me?"

I sighed. "I'm telling you that when it came to fighting, only one of us showed up for battle."

"Oh yeah? Who?" Tears filled her eyes like she knew the truth.

I leaned over her, kissed her forehead as if I was saying goodbye and whispered. "Me."

"That's not true! I would never—"

"Never say never. You have no idea what tragedy does to a person."

"Tragedy?" Her eyes were wild. "What tragedy? My accident?"

"Go." I swallowed the emotion in my throat. "Now."

"But Jax—"

"Go!" I roared, slamming my hands onto the table, knocking her plate from its place on the granite as it sailed to the floor in a loud crash.

Tears streamed down her face as she grabbed her purse and ran out of my apartment like I was the devil.

Sad part was.

Most days, that's exactly how my life felt.

Like Hell was on rewind.

And I had no way out.

II

Harley

I CRIED ALL the way to my car, big ugly tears that made my face feel hot and itchy and when I finally did make it to Grandma's to change, she was already taking her morning nap in front of the TV, remote in hand.

I tiptoed around, put on my yoga gear, and stopped in my room to just breathe.

"We're soup people."

I laughed and then giggled when he said, "I could use some soup."

"Nice ass that one." Grandma winked at me.

A headache pulsed between my eyes as I squeezed them shut. The voices and the memories came slowly, all taking place here in my room. My duvet was falling on the floor. I stared it down, searching for answers, and then I saw him there as if it was yesterday, shirtless, tugging me toward the mattress, hovering over me eagerness in his expression an almost boyish grin on his face. The guy didn't have a bad boy bone in his body, did he?

How did I know that?

What had shifted?

He was darker now, on the inside.

He had been so light then.

We were so light.

I let out a sigh and waited for more to come.

But I was grasping at air, trying to hold on to it, knowing it would just seep through my greedy fingers. There was so much more.

And he was a dick for not telling me.

Even if it was the worst news in the world, I deserved to know.

I wiped my tears one last time, put on a fresh coat of makeup like I was getting ready to go to war, and stared at myself in the mirror.

High ponytail.

Red lipstick.

Mascara.

Jax Romonov was messing with the wrong ex.

I stomped out of my room feeling lighter than I had in years, kissed Grandma's soft cheek, and drove like a bat out of hell all the way to the stadium.

One purpose in mind as I stomped down the hallways.

Without thinking, I opened up the locker room door where the guys changed and let myself in. It was the off-season, not like the whole team would be there, plus it felt right.

Like I used to do it all the time.

"Cover it up if you don't want to be laughed at or pointed at!" I yelled as guys quickly grabbed towels and clothing.

"Romonov!" One of the guys yelled. "Your woman's pissed!"

"My balls just shriveled," another guy muttered when I walked past.

I rolled my eyes and stopped right in front of Jax.

Our eyes locked.

He dropped his towel and smirked.

I gritted my teeth.

I would not look down. I would not be impressed. I would not lick my lips. I would not smolder. I would not waver.

But Holy Mother of God.

Mouth dry I waited for him to say something.

"Harley." He said my name in such an innocent, polite way that I wanted to smack him. "It's been hours since you left my place and you're still pissed?"

I felt my face heat.

Did he just declare we'd spent the night together?

In front of his entire team?

He crossed his arms.

I narrowed my eyes. "Well, maybe I'd be in a better mood if you knew what you were doing!"

"Dayum…" Sanchez said from behind me. I'd recognize that voice anywhere. My eyes flickered to the right, where Miller stood with a concerned look on his face. What? It's not any worse than what he said!

Jax's eyes moved into tiny slits as he stared down at me. "Look, if this is about me going out on a date tonight, you need to grow up."

Enraged, I shoved against his chest. "I'm not the one hiding shit!"

"I think everyone agrees I'm not hiding anything." He

spread his arms wide. Completely naked.

Ugh, what a jackass!

"Bro, you have a date?" Miller chimed in. "Since when?"

"Not now, Miller," Jax said through clenched teeth. "Now…" He turned back to me. "Would it kill you to just let it go and find your inner Elsa?"

"Yes." I gulped. "It just might."

"Everything okay in here?" One of the assistant coaches popped his head into the locker room.

I took a few steps back and nodded. Then I turned on my heel and left.

I just left.

The fight was in me.

But he was being purposely cruel, as if he was trying to shove me as far away from him as possible. But his eyes betrayed him.

His body language said go to hell.

His eyes said, you've always been my heaven.

"Now, just rest in downward dog for a few seconds, feel the stretch, and push back on your heels."

All the guys looked like they were enjoying themselves.

Every guy but Jax.

I decided to face away from the guys today, I didn't want to see his face, but every time I did a movement where I had to look under or behind me, his glare said it all.

He wanted to murder me.

Perfect, because I wanted to poison him.

And then ask him to kiss me.

And then cry a little bit.

Why did this have to be so hard?

Why did my brain have to be so broken? And why did it feel like my heart wasn't quite right, like the beats were out of cadence?

"That's it for today." My voice sounded uncertain and wobbly. I looked away when Sanchez seemed like he was about to ask if I was doing all right.

Miller walked up to me while I was gathering my things.

"So." His voice was gruff. "Jax told me you found out about the engagement."

The sting of tears burned both eyes. "Yeah, I may have gone a little crazy, yelled at him…"

Miller laughed. "He needs a little crazy in his life. I think he misses all the crazy."

I frowned. "Is that what I was?"

"No, you were more insane than crazy but in a really good way that changed him into a better man."

My heart leapt. "Care to fill in any details?"

"Oath of silence." He held up his hand. "Sanchez too. In fact, the whole team was told not to ruin your recovery, sorry."

"How the hell is that going to ruin my recovery?" I wondered out loud.

Miller eyed me up and down. "I'm not a doctor, but I could make an educated guess that any sort of mental shock to your system isn't going to be beneficial when your brain is already working really hard to fill in the spaces. Let it happen naturally, that's what the doctors said at least."

"It may never happen," I lamented.

"Then you need to move on," he said softly.

I looked up into his haunted eyes.

He knew.

They all knew!

It was like being part of a reality show only not being in on the actual project and assuming everything was real!

Miller put his hand on my shoulder and gave a light squeeze and then lifted it and walked off.

Jax stared at me across the small expanse of yoga mats and equipment and then he turned and gave me his back.

No.

NO.

Something was dying inside me.

Something big.

Something beautiful.

I ran at him, clearly without a plan, since the minute I was close enough to touch him, I jumped into his arms, not giving him time to think.

I slammed my mouth against his.

With a growl, he kissed me back so hard that he stumbled trying to hold on to me. I wrapped my legs around his waist. I lost myself in the kiss he gave me, and I prayed memories would surface as the feeling of his tongue pressed against mine made each heartbeat almost painful in my chest.

He tasted like good memories, bad ones too. He tasted like us.

Like what I was supposed to wake up to.

But there was more, such sadness in his kiss, in the way he shuddered. I clung to him for dear life

Dear God, please don't let me go. Please. Not this time.

His chest heaved as he pulled his mouth from mine, his eyes drilled into me. "You can't do that to me."

"Why?"

Slowly he pulled me from his body and sat me on my feet. "Because."

"You can't just say 'because'!" I yelled. "Tell me why, damn it! When there's this thing between us that's still there! Why?"

"Because it breaks my fucking heart!" he roared. "That's why!"

I stumbled back.

With tears in his eyes, he whispered. "And I don't have much of it left... so if you could please stop taking what working pieces I still have, I would appreciate it."

He walked off.

And I stood there stunned, feeling very much like I was the reason for all the bad in his life when maybe he had been the reason for all the good in mine.

Later that night I ignored the viral tweet of Jax smiling next to Noel.

I ignored the tears that constantly streamed down my face.

And I turned on the TV.

And let myself cry.

12

Jax

NOEL SMILED AT my side. We laughed during dinner, touched at least a dozen times right in front of the cameras like we usually did, but that was it.

People would assume whatever they wanted.

Harley would see.

And all would be well.

I pulled up to the large iron gate, typed in the code, then took the car down the long tree-lined driveway, stopping just in front of the obnoxious water fountain. "I had fun we should—"

"If you value your life, you won't finish that sentence with, 'do it again sometime,'" Noel said through clenched teeth. "Look, Jax, I get it, I do. We're using each other for a higher purpose or whatever, but you're miserable! I've never seen you like this even after—"

"If you value your life, you won't finish that sentence," I

parroted, knowing exactly what she would say. After the SIDS. After the breakup. After my heart stopped beating. "Look, I just need to make it through all the yoga shit. Then I won't be forced to see her all the time."

Noel clutched her white designer purse, her red shiny nails looking sharp and pristine against the leather. I chose to focus on that contrast instead of her pretty face, I knew I'd see disappointment there, and I was so tired of seeing that same look on every person I called friend.

So damn tired.

I would protect Harley until my dying day.

I'd sworn to her that much and more.

Sworn it to our child.

And I would keep that oath even if it killed me.

Pain lanced through my chest as I tried to suck in a breath.

"I'll text you. I have a benefit next week…" Noel said in a soft voice. Then she reached over and touched my thigh briefly before getting out of the car and slamming the door behind her.

Tears filled my eyes as I stared at the steering wheel.

It had been weeks since I'd been tempted.

But I was too broken, too damn weak because of her.

So, I gave in.

I opened my glove box, a little light turned on, and there it was, the last picture we had taken as a family.

I looked so fucking proud.

A dad.

A fiancé.

Smiling from ear to ear with a protective arm around my family. I remember thinking, I did this, I helped create this child. Who am I to deserve this life?

I wouldn't wish this on my worst enemy.

I swiped the tears on my cheeks, shut the glove box, and pulled the car out of park, my tires screeched as I drove back down the driveway. Belly laughs and giggles filled my head over and over again. I was so close to slipping.

To accidently pulling the steering wheel to the right as the bridge was coming up.

It would be front-page news.

America's Quarterback dies in a car accident but is reunited with his only reason for living.

More tears streamed down my cheeks.

I hadn't cried.

I refused to.

And now I couldn't stop it.

I couldn't fucking stop.

My eyes blurred as I hit the accelerator harder, going well over a hundred as I swerved to pass car after car.

My cell started ringing over the car speakers.

My finger hovered near the red end button on my dash.

Harley.

I hit the green and gripped the steering wheel with both hands as I bit out, "What?"

A few beats of silence and then. "You don't sound like yourself."

I snorted through my tears. "Yeah well, you would know, huh? Oh wait…"

"Stop being an ass."

"It's what I do best."

My tears were starting to dry on my cheeks, I looked to my right as the water beneath me tempted me to do the unthinkable.

I swerved.

And passed another car.

I was almost to the end of the bridge.

The moment seemed to trap me in time. It should have been seconds before I was past the water. It felt like an eternity. Painful memories flashed through my brain, ones that made my chest hurt and my muscles burn with indignation.

"It's not fair," I found myself saying with a crack to my voice. "It's not fucking fair!"

"What isn't? Jax? You seriously don't sound like yourself. I'm not trying to be mean, but I don't know, I just, God knows I'm so angry and confused, but I felt like I needed to call you, even though you push me away on a daily basis and yell at me in front of your teammates." She huffed into the phone. "This is ridiculous. What am I even doing?"

"I wanted to drive off the bridge." I said the words as I made my decision and kept my laser-like focus on the road. This was just another game.

Just another touchdown.

Only this time my opponent, my own worst enemy, was myself.

"Jax." Harley sounded like she was crying. "Please… I need you. Don't focus on anything else, all right? Just focus on my voice and drive home."

"Home," I repeated.

"I'll meet you at your apartment. Just stay on the phone with me, can you do that?"

"Yeah," I rasped. "I can do that."

I would look back on this conversation and remember nothing, not even the street lights, or the way the rain pelted my car like Seattle was experiencing its first hurricane. I wouldn't even remember pulling into my parking space and seeing Harley with her blue hoody and gray leggings standing there, face pale, much like the expression she had worn after the hospital that day when all was lost, when our girl died.

I got out of my car and stared at her.

At half of my world.

Knowing the other half was no longer with me.

How did people deal with this pain and not spontaneously combust? And not go crazy?

"Har—"

She slammed her body against mine, arms wrapped around my neck, legs around my waist, and then she pulled back and gripped my head between her hands. "The world needs you. I need you. If you ever pull that shit again, I'm not only going to kick your ass, I'm going to handcuff you to a loop in my jeans and throw away the key."

I smiled at that. "You rarely wear jeans."

"You tell me you want to jump off a bridge, I threaten to shadow you for the rest of your existence, and you choose to fixate on my clothing choices?" Tears spilled over onto her cheeks. "Please, Jax, please promise me, promise that—"

I kissed her. I had no idea what she wanted me to promise. And in that moment I didn't care. All I needed was to taste life.

Her life.

The life we shared.

Us.

I needed to feel like an us again, because I was doing a shit job at functioning as myself.

I tasted the salt of her tears as she deepened the kiss, her tongue fighting against mine for dominance as I turned around and pushed her against the car, angling my head for a deeper kiss, for more of her taste.

"Inside." She peppered kisses along my jawline. "Let's get inside."

"You go inside with me…" I swallowed thickly as I eyed her swollen lips. "You won't be leaving tonight."

"I'd rather stay home," she whispered. "With you."

13

Harley

I COULDN'T STOP shaking. His body was hot everywhere I touched, but it wasn't enough. I tried to get closer as he held me in his arms, as he refused to let me go in the elevator. My teeth chattered. I hated this, I hated that everything about him felt right and yet so broken between us, between a past I couldn't remember and one he wouldn't share with me.

All I knew is that if I lost him, if he walked out of my life, I wouldn't survive it, something inside me told me that I'd already been put through hell when it came to Jax, when it came to us.

I clung to him as the elevator lights flickered.

And instead of moving up... the elevator just stopped.

Lights flickered again.

And then we were blanketed in complete darkness.

I could feel his pulse beneath his skin, skyrocketing like mine, like maybe the universe needed to give us something else that was broken so we would find each other again, so we would stop dancing around the inevitable. The universe gave us a stalled elevator.

We had no place to run.

We had to face this.

Our demons.

Each other.

I inhaled his spicy scent and turned around in his arms and waited, one heartbeat, two. I counted a sigh from his lips, and I felt my body buzz with awareness at his closeness. Funny how I wasn't even worried about plummeting to my death, because I had Jax, and somehow that made everything okay. I was in his arms. Waiting, always waiting for him to make the move, to tell me everything, and then to follow it up with, *"It will be okay, I've got you."*

"Jax…" His name came out like a hoarse whisper as I clung to his wet T-shirt and felt his muscles beneath. "I need you the same way you need me."

His forehead touched mine. "I don't just need you, Harley. I can't seem to function without you."

"Charmer." My voice shook.

"I don't want to hurt you," he whispered against my mouth. I strained toward him, ready for more kissing, more of his hands rubbing up and down my arms. "But it doesn't matter anymore. I can't stay away. I'm going to hurt you, and I can't stop. I can't. You have to make me—"

I kissed him, then, and I tasted the yearning on his tongue, felt the need in his embrace as he returned my kiss and picked me up with one arm pressing my body against the cold wall of the elevator. My shirt went flying over my head while he drove his hips into me, deepening the kiss with velvet like strokes of his tongue. My hands dug into his wet hair as our mouths slid against one another, as our bodies fought for control when we both knew there was none to be found, not with us, not like this.

I didn't realize I was crying until he pulled back and swiped his thumbs across my cheeks and then kissed me tenderly down the neck, tugging at my leggings with his free hand. I squeezed my eyes shut as his mouth moved past my collarbone, his teeth grazed my bra strap as he tugged it down my right arm, and then my left. I prayed for the magical elevator to give us a few more minutes like this, where we didn't have to look into each other's eyes and see broken souls and promises. Maybe all we'd needed was darkness this whole time, a moment to just feel without really seeing and knowing there was so much more beneath this calm surface.

Chaos and truths unsaid swirled between us as I clung to him, digging my nails into his skin, needing to hang on as his fingers found my core. The last part of my leggings and underwear were tugged off my feet and thrown to the floor, I heard the drop with such finality that I let out a gasp.

This was happening.

Me and Jax.

The man I couldn't remember, but somehow still loved.

"I need you." He ducked his head into my neck and tensed. "Please."

"You have me." I gripped the sides of his face with my hands and pulled him down for a hungry kiss as he thrust into me. My legs wrapped around his narrow hips as he filled me. And for the first time since waking up in that hospital bed, I felt whole.

I was home.

He was my home.

Images of us laughing together, teasing, filled my brain on such overdrive that I had a hard time placing them with the feeling of rightness as he pumped into me, my head fell back against the wall hitting it hard enough for me to wince, and then more images as he drove forward with a curse.

"Needed you so bad." He gripped my ass with his hands.

"Jax!" I clung to him, afraid this was a dream and he'd let go, I didn't want it to end. I could feel him everywhere, see him in my mind, this was familiar, us together, frantic.

Always frantic.

"Soup." Jax grinned at me. "I could do soup."

The conversation was like watching a movie on repeat. And then we were both standing in his apartment and we were in his bed having sex, no condom, and I remember not caring, thinking this is the man I'm going to spend the rest of my life. I know he's clean. And if I get pregnant, maybe his dad…

Jax's dad.

Wait.

Jax let out another curse as his hips pumped faster.

I felt my release coming too fast, I needed to stay in this moment, to remember, I needed to remember. I held back, felt his frustration as his fingers moved between us.

No.

I shook my head back and forth.

"I give you my blessing…" His father was on his death bed.

They took shots at his funeral.

Why didn't I take a shot?

I'm back in Jax's apartment. I'm touching my belly and laughing while Jax throws something across the baby's room and yells how the directions are wrong.

We christen the room.

And I'm back in the present, with the love of my broken life, in his arms finally letting go feeling him chase me, body shaking.

I slid down the elevator wall and hung my head in my hands. "I remember."

Jax went completely still. All I could hear was his heavy breathing and the tension in the elevator as the lights flickered back on and we started moving.

I was half naked on the floor. His eyes were bloodshot as he stared at me, motionless like a pretty statue.

"I remember everything."

Jax turned and rammed his fist into the elevator wall and hung his head. "I wish I was dead too."

14

Jax

I WAS BREATHING hard.

Frantic.

Heartbroken.

Harley looked up at me, not with thankfulness in her eyes but sheer betrayal. She pressed her fingers to her forehead, licked her swollen lips, and then reared back and punched me in the chest.

"Shit!" She shook her fist and started jumping up and down.

I deserved that. "Are you okay?"

"No, Jax!" she screamed. "I'm not okay! "I'm trapped on an elevator with the father of my dead child, and the memories keep coming like a freight train, my brain hurts, my heart is broken, and you want to know if I'm all right?"

This was what I had tried to prevent.

This is why I should have stayed away.

I hung my head. "Har—"

"Don't you 'Har' me You kept this from me!"

I glared at her, barely making out her face in the dim lighting. "I vowed to always love you, to always keep you safe. I promised our little girl—" I choked on the sob that wanted to release. "I promised her I'd do everything in my power to make sure you didn't bear this burden alone, and the minute you're finally able to breathe because you don't feel like the news of her death is suffocating you to death every waking hour — you say I kept it from you?"

She shoved against me. I caught her by the arms, and then she was trying to hit me again, her hands flew at my chest, my face.

Finally, I just wrapped my massive arms around her and held her tight. "Stop, Har. It won't make you feel better. Trust me nothing will make it feel better."

"We were supposed to be a team," she finally said in a harsh whisper. "You and me… and you made me think I was crazy, like I was losing my mind over this empty feeling I've had since the accident." She gasped. "It's been a year of lies, Jax! Why didn't anyone say anything? Grandma? Our friends?"

"A year where you didn't wake up sobbing in my arms, yes," I answered softly. "I made them promise, and in the end the doctors said that it could shock you too much that it could be harmful, so they let me give you the lie. A year, Harley, a year since you woke up sobbing in my arms."

"I did that," she admitted.

"Every night," I added. "And you needed someone to blame, Har, we both did. It ripped us apart. Our love was stripped from us the minute she left this earth."

Harley burst into tears. "She was so small."

"She was perfect."

"And she wasn't crying. She slept through the night, I was so relieved." She started to cry harder. "Because I'd been so tired, and I just wanted a break. I could have saved her, Jax, I could have—"

"No." I cupped her chin. "Look at me."

I could barely make out her eyes, but I felt her tears slide down her cheeks, hitting me, stripping my emotions bare with each drop.

"It wasn't your fault. Don't you see? That's the only reason I let you walk out that door was because I knew you needed someone to blame, and I love you too much for you to take that on. Blame me, blame God, blame the damn apartment being too stuffy, or the crib being too big for her, blame all of the above." I swallowed hard, forcing my sorrow down before it choked me. "Just don't blame yourself, all right? Don't."

She pressed her forehead to my chest as the elevator shuddered. But it kept traveling slowly upward... to the apartment we used to share together.

To the life we should have had.

Except we were empty, both of us.

Broken.

Our hearts severed because we were missing a little girl with wispy blonde curls and blue eyes.

I squeezed my eyes shut as the elevator doors opened.

Harley was still clinging to me when we walked side by side to the apartment. I shoved the key in the door lock, turned it.

And that feeling was back.

The one that reminded me that everything was the same, and yet so different.

At least Harley could move on.

At least she would know why.

I could taste her still, wanted her more than my next breath.

I didn't deserve her.

I needed to be the strong one, the one who took the fall. That's what my dad would have done, that's what he taught me. I was the superhero of the scenario, and she deserved to be happy.

She pulled away from me.

I gritted my teeth and waited for the inevitable.

She walked to the middle of the living room, and then turned her head toward the hall.

I knew what she was thinking.

No noise.

Why did silence piss me off so much?

Because at least when she was crying, I knew she was alive.

"I just wanted sleep," Harley said in a whisper I barely heard. "She was dying, and I was sleeping."

"Harley." I stomped over to her and grabbed her by the elbow, forcing her to look at me. "You need to stop! The doctors said there was nothing we could have done, nothing! Hate me, blame me, yell at me, but don't let that guilt fester in your soul. You were sleeping and so was she. The only difference is, you woke up, and she went to Heaven." My voice cracked.

Damn it, the pain was still so raw.

Harley burst into tears all over again. "At least she wasn't in pain."

"Sweetheart." I wrapped my arms around her trembling frame and held her close. "What was the last thing you did with her before putting her down?"

She clung to my shirt, twisting it in her hands. "I sang her

Twinkle, Twinkle." She sobbed harder. "And I told her to reach for the stars."

I squeezed my eyes shut as fresh tears poured down my cheeks. "And Harley, she did, our little girl did. She reached, and she was happy, so fucking happy." So were we.

"I yelled at you." Harley's voice was so heavy with sadness I just wanted to keep holding her in my arms and ask her to give it to me, the burden, the grief, all of it. It had been over a year, and I was still mourning the loss of her.

I couldn't even bring myself to say her name out loud.

Harley pulled away from me, walked into the kitchen, jumped up on the counter, and grabbed the giant stash of candy I kept in my cupboard above the fridge.

She reached for a bottle of rum.

And then she moved to the couch and set everything down. She flopped down and started drinking straight from the bottle, following that with a healthy bite out of a Hershey bar.

"Clearly everything's coming back to you if you're chugging rum and eating chocolate."

It was one of my favorite things about her. The fact that she didn't give a shit. She was unapologetically herself. If she wanted chocolate, she didn't weigh it or say she was going to skip dessert for a week so she could have it. She just opened the damn candy bar and made it her bitch.

The same with rum.

Life, according to Harley, was meant to be lived.

Tentatively, I walked over to the couch and sat down.

She handed me a Snickers bar.

I shoved it in my mouth and chewed. Chocolate sweetness melted on my tongue, and I almost moaned out loud, it tasted so good.

Next came the bottle of rum.

I took two swigs and reveled in the smooth burn as it went down. I handed the bottle back.

And then I was buzzed enough to blurt, "I missed you."

She stood, held out her hand, and led me to the bedroom we used to share.

Without speaking, we moved around the room, I shed my clothes down to my boxer briefs and tossed her a white T-shirt. She grabbed it midair and pulled it over her sports bra. I caught the flash of black boy short panties.

And then we crawled into bed.

She flipped on the ID channel.

I kissed her head.

And still without speaking… we eventually, fell asleep.

15

Harley

I was sick with sadness.

It felt like my heart was rotting inside my body, like someone was drowning me in my own tears, making it so I couldn't suck in the air I needed.

I jolted awake.

Her smile filled my line of vision.

We'd gotten pregnant accidentally.

And then the happy accident turned into this amazing miracle. Jax was the best father. So patient, so helpful when it came to feedings since I didn't produce enough milk.

He took the night shift.

He let me sleep.

And then pre-season had started. He wanted me to get a nanny to help, and I told him I could do it on my own and he could kiss my ass.

Slowly I'd gotten more and more exhausted. He tried to

help, he sent a masseuse to the apartment once a week, and said he was going to start interviewing nannies so I could at least shower during the day. I was so absorbed in being the perfect mom to the perfect family that I lost myself a bit. I wasn't showering as much as normal, and I was sad, so sad. And I couldn't figure out why I was so sad when I had everything.

I was living the dream.

Engaged to the hottest quarterback in the NFL.

With a precious little child.

Whom I resented.

That was my secret.

That was my guilt.

Something was broken in me.

Because I didn't feel like I was the same after giving birth. The rooms felt darker, the universe altered. I didn't feel like me.

So, I faked it.

And I resented Jax when he left for practice.

And then I felt guilt when he'd come home and make it look so easy.

And then she would cry and I would cry, and then I would hold her and realize how much I loved her, and how much I loved us.

The last few days of her life were the happiest of mine.

Jax noticed something was off, but he never said anything. I could see him watching me as though perplexed sometimes.

And I finally decided that I needed to talk to someone, a therapist. I did one of those online consultations where you Skype, and she immediately told me what was wrong.

I had postpartum depression.

Time helped heal, but also I was my own worst enemy.

With my need to prove myself to Jax, to the world, that I could do this and I could rock it, I was killing myself. My emotional health wasn't what it should be.

Once I realized it wasn't the new normal, that it wasn't my perfect child, but a mixture of projection, fear, resentment, hormones changing, and shock, I finally let myself go.

That's when I started singing her to sleep at night.

It was our time.

Special.

And that night, I went to bed thinking, wow, all we needed was time.

And I woke up without the knowledge that I had no time left.

"Hey." Jax pulled me into his arms. "You've been crying again."

"I had postpartum," I blurted, my eyes finding the alarm clock that said four a.m. "I was so angry at you, how easy you made it look, how perfect you were at just… everything. And I was so tired, Jax, and I was trying so hard." I shook my head. "And I wasn't myself, I wasn't."

"Shhhh." He pulled me onto his lap. "Har, I know you weren't yourself. I knew it then, but I also knew that the more I pushed, the more you pulled away."

"I blamed you," I admitted. "Because I tried so hard and still felt like I failed, and because I was finally feeling better, and then this happened and I couldn't take it, Jax. My heart couldn't take it."

"I know."

"Stop being so understanding and yell at me!" I tried shoving against his chest. It was futile, the man had the best guns in the business.

"You done struggling?" he whispered against my neck.

"Maybe." I leaned back against him, sinking into his hard body, loving the way he protectively held me, making himself a shield against the world. "I don't deserve you."

"Stop." His command was harsh. "I'm the one that kept this from you for a year, Harley. I just — I knew you had a second chance at life, a second chance at happiness without seeing the memory of her in my eyes."

"I messed up," I whispered.

"We both did."

Without even knowing it, I had missed the way he held on to me with such strength. He'd been everything to me, who was I kidding? He still was.

He was all I had left.

He wasn't just my past.

He was my future.

No matter how painful it was to think about, to look into his blue eyes and know that hers had been identical... he was what I had left.

And it was time to pick up the pieces, wasn't it?

"I don't forgive you yet." I turned in his arms and locked eyes with him. "You pushed me away for a year, and I struggled on my own—"

"Harley I—"

He stopped talking, and his face flashed with such intense pain I wanted to pull him in for a hug and never let go.

"Listen." I gripped the sides of his face. "You need to promise me, no matter how ugly, how painful, how horrible things get, that you don't shield me from them, you don't make decisions on our behalf, you let me get a vote. Otherwise this isn't going to work. Ever."

His eyes searched mine. "Are you saying you're willing to forgive me?"

I waited a few seconds then rasped, "Yes. If you'll have me—"

He kissed the sentence away, gripped me by the ass, and threw me down on the mattress. Sigh. Football players.

So aggressive these days.

A little helmet to helmet action, meaning his forehead was pressed against mine as he tugged down my boy shorts and threw them to the side. "You won't be needing those."

"I won't be needing those," I agreed with a wide smile as he pulled up the cotton T-shirt and threw it on the foot of the bed.

"That either."

"Agreed." I bit down on my lower lip to keep from smiling like a fool as he leaned over my body, his hands roaming up and down my sides like he was memorizing me all over again and taking mental pictures of how perfect we were together, how perfect we'd always been.

"I love you, Harley." He kissed me softly, the hard weight of his body had me squeezing my eyes shut with pleasure as he slid into me, effortlessly pinning me against the mattress, holding me there, exhaling against my neck as he whispered in my ear. "I'm never letting you go."

"Just feed me and let me have bathroom breaks, and you have a deal," I teased.

"Ah, already negotiating." He rolled his hips.

I let out a little shriek. "Hmmm, yes?"

Jax grinned down at me his mouth finding mine as his body continued to move, creating waves of pleasure that had my soul flying off the bed into the universe while my body was still beneath his. "The next time you walk out that door it's with an empty suitcase, and when you walk back in, it's for good, and I want that suitcase fucking full."

Tears welled in my eyes. It was almost too much. Jax was everywhere, inside me, pleasuring me, his hands touching me, the heat of his gaze searing me in place.

This beautiful man was mine.

And no matter what pain stood between us, at least it reminded us that we were alive, that we got that chance, that we owed it to our little girl to live and to love each other through the sorrow.

"I love you, Harley." I felt his huge body still, like he was trying to hold back.

Always such a gentleman, my quarterback.

"I love you too." I yanked his head down for a kiss and whispered against his lips. "Let go."

"You first."

"Together."

"Always," he rasped.

I'll never forget the way it felt.

Finding my way back home.

In his arms.

16

Jax

Pre-season
Bellevue Bucks vs. Seattle Sharks

"SHE HAS FRESH flowers," Harley said in an awestruck voice.

"Every week." I shrugged like it wasn't a big deal. "I bring fresh flowers every week for my dad, and I bring fresh flowers for her."

Tears welled in her eyes. "I love that they're buried side by side."

I pulled her close. "I love that she has a papa in Heaven."

She turned her face into my chest and let the tears fall. "You think he sings her Twinkle Twinkle?"

"I think he holds her while she sleeps." I admitted. "I think I can feel them sometimes, laughing with each other. I can still hear her giggle, and I wonder if the greatest gift in my dad's death was that he would be there paving the way for when she went to meet him in Heaven."

Harley pulled away from me and sank to her knees in front

of the tiny grave that no parent should ever have to lay flower on.

Daisy Rose.

"Beloved daughter, our joy." Harley read the tombstone then laid down yellow daisies, "Your dad and I found each other again. It only took a severe head wound on my part and complete stubbornness on his, but we'll try, for you we're trying. Our love made you and our love for you will keep us close forever, I promise."

I put my hand on Harley's shoulder and helped her to her feet, then dropped to my knees in front of our little girl's grave. "I want you to be my wife, I want our little girl to see her mom and dad happy, together, laughing again, I want us to try for more little girls when the time's right, and I want her to be proud."

"Yes." Harley squeezed her eyes shut as tear after tear dripped off her chin. "Yes!"

I shoved a new ring on her finger, not the one she'd seen before, but one that held new meaning. I got to my feet, still watching her.

Maybe she noticed a difference in the feel or something, because she finally looked down and burst into tears.

I was a gold daisy with a giant diamond in the middle of it, antique cut, and tiny little roses etched along the band.

"It's her." She said reverently, staring at it.

"Because she brought us back," I said simply. "And because she'll always be part of what's special between us."

"God, I love you Jax Romonov!" She launched herself into my arms.

I caught her and swung her around. "I love you too."

"Okay." She pulled away, sighed, and wiped her tears.

"Now it's time, now I'm ready."

"Oh, you're ready?" I teased.

"Yes." She beamed. "Daisy and your dad will cheer from heaven, and I'll take care of things down here. Throw an interception and I'm withholding sex for two days."

My face hardened. "You wouldn't do that to a man."

"We can't lose," came her response.

I let out a groan and led her back to the SUV. "Seriously? Just like that?"

"It's the pre-season opener, I can't have my man throwing interceptions. Your concentration has been complete shit, even Sanchez says so."

"I feel ganged up on." I muttered, starting the car and driving us toward the stadium. I needed to get there a few hours early and I didn't want to let Harley out of my sight.

Things had been good.

Better than good.

We still fought. Then again, I would think something was wrong if she wasn't stealing my toothbrush or hiding my candy stash.

It felt better.

But it still hurt.

This was the first day she'd wanted to come to the grave. I understood her reasons for not wanting to see the cold hard ground and the marble gray tombstone above it. It still wreaked havoc on my soul when I visited.

But I was a dad.

And dads took care of their little girls.

So I went.

Every week.

This was the first time the weight had lifted, just slightly, maybe because I had my other half with me, and I wasn't facing the grief all by myself, and I wasn't taking all the blame like I had before. She was communicating with me, and she was laughing again.

She was in my arms again.

I wanted it to stay that way forever.

Which was probably why I was already sweating.

"You okay?" Harley asked once we made it to the stadium and parked.

"Totally," I lied as she looked around and frowned. "What?"

"It's completely packed." She waved her hand around. She was in a black and white Bellevue Bucks jersey, mine obviously. She had two little streaks of black under each eye and a temporary Bucks tattoo on her right cheek. Her leggings were the typical white and black streaked and she had on her pink Nikes. One of my favorite Bucks beanies covered part of her head, and in that moment I realized she'd never looked more beautiful.

With my ring on her finger.

In my gear.

Grinning from ear to ear.

"Yeah well, it's a big game." I shrugged it off and exhaled roughly before going to her side of the car and opening the door.

She stepped out and wrapped an arm around me. I kept my bag on my right and walked with her toward the back door through which the players entered.

We were right on time.

I checked my Rolex and tried to get the jitters out.

"You ready?" I reached for the door.

Harley gave me a funny look and crossed her arms, her dark

hair spilled over her right shoulder. God, she was pretty. Her eyes gazed into mine. "You never get nervous before games. And it's pre-season. You won't even play the whole time."

"Maybe I'm nervous that you're going to be watching and refused to give me sex if I throw an interception."

I jerked the door open.

Sanchez blocked the way. "She's withholding if you do what?"

I let out a sigh. "How did you even hear that?"

"Bro, I was standing right here, and I'm happy to say you're right on time. If you'll just drop your bag and head on out, I'll stay here with Harley."

"What?" Harley looked between us.

Sanchez winked, the bastard, too good looking to be touching her, but such a great receiver I put up with his shit. Plus he was a friend, hell he was family.

I ran down the hall and out the tunnel where the crowd was waiting. And it was a big crowd. Typically people watched us play before the game, but we'd let all the players' families know what was happening as well as a few close friends.

I was wearing a suit like I always did on game day. Today it was a three-piece gray pinstripe that made me feel like I belonged in Men's Journal. Miller was wearing a red vest with gray, and he gave me a wink when I jogged to him mid-field.

Kinsey and Emerson were in similar gear to Harley, both stood on the left while Miller stood on the right.

Sanchez soon appeared and joined us while the team chaplain, Dirk, jogged over and stood in the middle.

"Ready?" he asked.

"Yes." I was going to lose my mind if she panicked, but I didn't want to wait. She'd said yes, and I wanted to start this season off with my wife at my side. It was time.

"Good thing she didn't say no, yeah?" Sanchez elbowed Miller.

Miller just rolled his eyes. "Really? Now?"

The bridal march started.

And a teary-eyed Harley appeared on the arm of her grandmother, who had on her own jersey and hat.

They walked slowly toward us.

Harley had a bouquet of blue daisies in her hand, our daughter's hospital bracelet wrapped around the stems.

My eyes filled with tears as she made her way toward us.

My teammates flanked the aisle way, friends and family members all grinning ear to ear, as my coaching staff looked on and the stadium started to cheer.

She finally made it to me.

"You mad?" I whispered, taking her hand from her grandmother's and kissing her on her cheek.

"I'm only mad we didn't do this months ago." Her eyes beamed at me, and then I grabbed her hand.

She placed it on the bouquet.

Both of our fingers grazed the hospital bracelet.

And I could have sworn when we said I do, a gentle breeze picked up, and the smell of daisies filled the air.

It was right.

Our story wasn't beautiful.

It was filled with obliterating pain.

But the thing with life is this: pain doesn't last forever. There will always be a gentle breeze to soothe away the sting, and you may just find that you're a little bit stronger than before, a little braver, and a lot more willing to live life as it should be lived. Fearlessly.

"You may now kiss the bride!" Dirk announced.

Harley being Harley jumped into my arms, wrapped her legs around me, and kissed me against the mouth, her tongue not even pretending to stay away from mine, her front rubbing against my suit.

It was perfect.

It was us.

The crowd cheered while Kinz and Emerson wiped tears from their eyes and then Harley pulled back and laughed. "Does that mean we get hot dogs now?"

Sanchez burst out laughing. "You get his ho—"

"Finish that sentence, I dare you," I said without looking at him, causing more laughter amongst the group. "You, Harley Romonov, get whatever you want."

I would go home that night after a win.

I would walk with my wife to the room I had refused to clean.

I would sit with her and cry.

And then, slowly, we would heal together.

Two Years Later

"P<small>USH</small>!" D<small>OCTOR</small> S<small>NYDER</small> encouraged.

Harley gave me a look of pure murder.

"Baby," I grabbed her hands. "You have to push."

"YOU PUSH!" she roared.

I jerked back, eyes wide. The woman was possessed!

"Harley," the doc tried again, his voice calm and firm. "Just one more, all right?"

She squeezed her eyes shut and pushed.

And then I saw him.

The most beautiful baby boy in the entire universe.

"Good job, Mama," I whispered in her hair.

The doc handed me the scissors to cut the cord, and then I was holding my son, and placing him on Harley's chest.

She burst into tears. "He's perfect."

"He is."

And then I frowned as I looked at his little foot and saw the tiniest birthmark.

In the shape of a daisy.

Harley gasped.

I couldn't speak.

The doctor probably thought we were insane when we both cried over our little boy and something that so many parents would think was a beauty mark or at most a minor blemish, when we knew the truth.

The universe had given us another gift, a fresh start, and quite possibly a sign from heaven that said, *"I love you."*

WANT MORE RVD?

Check out these excerpts from All Stars Fall & Risky Play!

ALL STARS FALL
A Seaside Pictures Novel/Kristin Proby Crossover
STANDALONE

I woke up the next morning to a pounding headache and Bella sitting on my chest asking for peanut butter pancakes. Something flew into my room. A ball? A spaceship? Who knew at this point?

And then crying.

All the crying.

"He hit me!" Bella wailed and wrapped her arms around my neck. I just laid there staring up at the ceiling wondering how I was messing it up so horribly. Josie had a lot of faults, but at least she'd been a good stay-at-home mom, until she couldn't handle the fact that I was touring for an entire year, leaving her in the dust.

Her words, not mine.

She left me the night of the Grammys.

I got a Grammy, and she walked out of my life because she was jealous.

I saw it for what it was.

Knew several Hollywood couples who said the very reason they never dated or married someone in the same industry was because you were always competing for roles, fame, Instagram followers.

I held on to Bella until she stopped crying.

"All better?" I asked in my raspy sleep-filled voice. I'd at least gotten five hours last night. I needed to lay some more tracks. Each of the guys had taken a much-needed break and decided to drop a solo album.

Our manager was thrilled.

Our agent was swimming in money.

And since I owned my own studio back in Malibu, I'd known it would be easy to do, except now I wasn't so sure.

What was I supposed to do? Take the kids with me on tour? They'd done a few cities with me last year, but I didn't want to take them out of school.

With a deep breath, I heaved Bella into the air and threw my feet over the side of the bed, landing on a few misplaced Legos that had my eyes watering and curse words screaming inside my head.

"Daddy hurt?" Bella cupped my face.

"A bit," I lied. Son of a bitch, I was going to get rid of every last Lego in that house. "Just… give me a minute."

"Your face is red," she pointed out with a grin, damn her and those dimples. "Are you saying crap in your head?"

I had told her crap was a bad word that adults said when they were angry and that if she was really *really* angry, she could use it like her brothers.

Yes, the answer is yes; it has backfired one hundred percent.

"Boys!" I called downstairs while Malcom and Eric chased each other around the island in the kitchen. "Get the pancake mix out!"

They grumbled.

More things were thrown.

Chaos. I lived in absolute chaos.

Exhausted, even though the day was just starting, I carried Bella down the stairs and started in on the pancakes, all the while staring at the clock with relief. Three hours. In three hours, the new nanny would be here.

Fingers crossed the twins didn't set her on fire.

And maybe she'd braid Bella's hair again.

My gut clenched.

I'd felt like a complete idiot staring at the pretty barista with my jaw hanging to the floor. She'd wrangled in my kids faster than I did. They reacted to her in a way I hadn't seen in a really long time.

It had been such a relief that for a minute all I could do was stare. She had flawless, makeup-free skin, and her hair was in this adorable knot at the top of her head. I couldn't tell if she was in her early twenties or late. Maybe all the Botox I'd been exposed to in LA was messing with my head. I hated guessing ages because I was almost always wrong. Look at the ex.

"Dad?" Eric interrupted my thoughts.

"Yeah, buddy?" I snapped out of it and grabbed a mixing bowl.

"You're smiling awful big over pancakes."

Little shit. I stared him down and winked. "That's because I'm adding chocolate chips!"

"Hooray!" Bella squealed in delight while Malcom and Eric gave each other high fives then grabbed their iPads and sat at the breakfast bar.

Coffee.

Would it be wrong to train my children how to make me coffee so that I at least had a cup waiting when I woke up to multiple screams, tears, and flying objects?

I heaved a sigh. It would probably have seven Legos and a booger.

At this point, I would take it all and say God bless you every one.

I grabbed a pod for the Keurig, yawned, and made myself

a cup while Bella tried mixing the batter. She had more outside the bowl than inside, but she liked to stir.

She started helping cook when she was two.

And couldn't say stir to save her life, which only meant I stared at her like an idiot until she grabbed a spoon. "Sway sway sway!"

That was her word for stir.

It was a conundrum.

At least she was helpful while her brothers literally watched other children play with toys on YouTube.

Something was very wrong with people in this world if that was a thing. I watched one episode of a guy singing Best Friend Best Friend while opening candy and nearly called the police.

Because if that doesn't scream pedophile, then I really don't know what does.

Coffee brewed, and pan on, I grabbed the bowl from Bella and started to pour out the pancakes.

I felt slightly guilty when I eyed the clock again.

My fingers twitched with the need to play out my frustration on the drums, with the need to write music and send it to the guys to see if it was good enough. And on top of that, I had the band AD2 coming in at the end of the week to lay two tracks.

Technically, they lived here only during the summer months, but now that Alec, the older brother, had a kid with another one on the way, they were thinking about staying permanently because of schools.

My plate was full.

And I was ready to offer the new nanny a million dollars plus benefits if she'd just clean up the Legos.

That was when you knew you were at your limit — when you would pay a complete stranger to pick up the hazardous toys sprinkled around your house like miniature bombs ready to go off.

"ERIC!" Malcom screamed. "STOP TOUCHING ME!"

I chugged my coffee, burning my tongue in the process, and eyed the clock again. Two and a half hours, I could last two and a half hours. Right?

RISKY PLAY

"Where are you staying, Ashley?" Hugo asked.

Oh duh, me. He was talking to me. I was Ashley, not Mackenzie. "Um, the Secrets resort, something…" I frowned. All I could remember was that I'd booked the penthouse with a swim-out because Alton said he'd want his own private pool for us since we wouldn't be leaving the room at all.

I blushed at the thought.

Funny, since the guy had never passed third base the entire time we were together.

Saving it for later, he said.

Making it special, he said.

He respected my father too much, he said.

Hugo handed me my bag. "Me too."

"You too?" I said in a confused voice as we were shuffled out of the plane by security and enough police officers to make my head dizzy.

"Secrets," he said slowly. "It was one of the first ones to pop up on my search engine. I booked it and didn't look back."

"Oh." My head felt warm as I followed him off the plane and toward customs. He went into a different line, not that I was watching.

By the time my passport was stamped and I found my luggage, he was nowhere to be found.

I tried not to be disappointed.

After all, this vacation was about me.

Not the handsome stranger I'd kissed in first class when I thought I was about to die.

"You ready?" Hugo said from behind.

I jerked and then turned as he dangled the keys to what looked like a Ferrari — the rearing horse emblem was a dead giveaway — in front of my face.

I was used to money.

But my family didn't spend it if it wasn't necessary.

So renting an expensive foreign car?

Not necessary when you could invest!

Who was this guy?

"You're not one of those people that kidnap Americans and then get a ransom, are you?" I asked stupidly.

He bit down on his lip. "Do I look like a kidnapper?"

"Well…" I narrowed my eyes and studied him. "No. Yes. I'm not sure."

He leaned in until we were chest to chest. "Trust me."

I sucked in a breath, he was so close, and the gold flecks in his eyes were so hypnotic I didn't even blink. "Can I?"

He shrugged. "Who knows? You're being spontaneous, you're the one with all the regrets."

"Not true—" I started to argue.

He silenced me with a brief kiss that left me shocked, aroused, and my heart pounding. "Then why the question? The one thing you ask before you plummet to your death is what you would do different, which makes me assume you would do a lot of things different, and you don't look like the type of girl who gets into cars with strange men."

"That's because I listened about stranger danger in school." I smirked.

He barked out a laugh. "I must have missed that lesson." One side of his mouth lifted in a cocky half smile. "I skipped a lot of school…"

"Shocking." I crossed my arms.

"Get in."

"But—"

"Send a text to your mom, dad, best friend."

I tried not to cringe at the words best friend.

"Let them know where you are and where you're going just in case you really don't trust me, then get in the damn car."

He was already taking my bags when I texted my mom my location and turned on my GPS.

And then I was suddenly sitting with a complete stranger in a sexy electric-blue Ferrari that roared to life so hard and fast I almost felt sorry that we couldn't just take it out for a few hours. Then again, he was a stranger. Would it be weird to ask for a joyride? Something told me that's how good girls get kidnapped or end up pregnant, sports cars and guys who look like that.

Hugo put on a pair of black Ray-Bans and grinned over at me. "You ready for vacation?"

"Ready." I wasn't ready. I so wasn't ready. This wasn't me. This behavior. But something was building in my chest, something exciting, something that felt both wrong and right at the same time.

He hit the accelerator.

I let out a scream as we flew out of the airport and down the streets of Puerto Vallarta. We passed malls, restaurants, car dealerships, and finally about ten minutes into our trip he turned right then left, and there we were.

Secrets.

The guard at the gate asked for our passports, then widened his eyes for a brief minute before Hugo slipped something into his hand and fired off something in Spanish.

The man grinned and held out his phone.

Hugo turned to me. "He wants to take a picture of us on our first day. I may have lied and said we were married..."

My face fell.

"It will be quick, promise. No worries."

Before I knew what was happening, I was leaning in and taking a picture with Hugo, and then I was being helped out of the car and handed a glass of champagne.

The staff seemed a little eager to see us arrive.

Maybe it was the car?

Hugo seemed to calm everyone down with a few gorgeous words in Spanish. I even found myself nodding, though I couldn't understand a word because he was talking so fast. I could only catch enough to know he was discussing his stay and something else about a newspaper.

I'd stupidly studied French all through college.

That, I was fluent in. But Spanish? Nada.

Okay, so I knew nothing.

Literally.

In seconds, I was swept away to registration. Across the room, Hugo was making sweeping motions with his hands while a little kid ran up and tossed him a soccer ball.

I frowned.

The ladies at registration kept pointing and covering their mouths with their hands while they giggled.

Yeah, I got it, I did.

The man was gorgeous.

Not merely "Oh look, he has nice eyes and a body that could run for days without breaking a sweat," but really just... beautiful to look at.

All smooth skin, rippling forearm muscles, and bracelets

— how did a guy get away with wearing so many different rope bracelets without looking stupid?

I blinked and looked closer. Did he have a braid in his hair too?

Huh.

The same silky hair I'd tugged on.

I shivered.

"Welcome home!" Marta said with a grin. "You've booked the penthouse suite for four days. Anything you need at all, and we'll have a butler personally see to it, Miss—" I grabbed my key cards before she could say my name.

"Thank you!" I interrupted and stood. "I'm tired, I think I'll just go—" I did a 360. "Where's the elevator?"

"I'll go with you." Hugo flashed me his key card.

"Hmm, you following me now?" I teased.

"Apparently we both have good taste." He flashed his key card and packet; there were two penthouse suites per floor.

Side by freaking side.

I was P601.

And he was P602.

I shook my head; it was ridiculous, wasn't it?

These things didn't really happen, did they?

The elevator dinged at our level, and we stepped off. "I'm just going to…" I pointed to my door.

"Nap? Relax? Drink?" he offered.

"Yeah, all of the above," I admitted.

"See you around, then." I felt his smile make its way down my body like a caress and then experienced extreme disappointment after I slid my key card and was met with emptiness when the door opened.

This was supposed to be our room.

Our honeymoon.

Filled with champagne and sex, that was what you did on a honeymoon, right?

Like I would even know.

I walked out to the balcony and swim-out pool as the sound of waves crashing against the sand filled my ears.

A chilled bottle of champagne waited with chocolate-covered strawberries.

"Congratulations, Mr. and Mrs. Davis!"

I ripped the card in half, then in thirds, then momentarily lost my mind and imagined setting it on fire, when a voice called out. "Great view, huh?"

Hugo was literally my neighbor except for a partition that blocked him from seeing my pool and into my room.

I gulped and looked out at the ocean. "Yeah, it is."

"More champagne?" He pointed to my hand still clutching the champagne with a vise-like grip.

"Yeah," I croaked.

"Are you by yourself?" he asked a few seconds later.

"Yes." Don't cry. Don't cry. Don't cry.

"Do you want to be?" he asked softly.

I shook my head, no…

Just then he hopped over the partition, swept me into his arms, and lowered his head. His mouth was searing hot, his grip tender like he knew my shame, my sadness, and wanted to make them go away the only way he knew how. I clung to that kiss like a lifeline and promised myself I'd do whatever it took to forget Alton — and be the girl of adventure I'd always wanted to be.

I was going to start with Hugo.

ABOUT THE AUTHOR

RACHEL VAN DYKEN is a *New York Times, Wall Street Journal*, and *USA Today* bestselling author. When she's not writing about hot hunks for her Regency romance or New Adult fiction books, Rachel is dreaming up *new* hunks. (The more hunks, the merrier!) While Rachel writes a lot, she also makes sure she enjoys the finer things in life — like *The Bachelor* and strong coffee.

Rachel lives in Idaho with her husband, son, and two boxers. Fans can follow her writing journey at www.RachelVanDykenAuthor.com and www.facebook.com/rachelvandyken.

ALSO BY RACHEL VAN DYKEN

Cruel Summer
Summer Heat
Summer Seduction
Summer Nights

The Consequence Series
The Consequence of Loving Colton
The Consequence of Revenge
The Consequence of Seduction
The Consequence of Rejection

Wingmen Inc.
The Matchmaker's Playbook
The Matchmaker's Replacement

The Bachelors of Arizona
The Bachelor Auction
The Playboy Bachelor
The Bachelor Contract

Curious Liaisons
Cheater
Cheater's Regret

Players Game
Fraternize
Infraction
MVP

Liars, Inc
Dirty Exes
Dangerous Exes

RACHEL VAN DYKEN BOOKS

www.rachelvandykenauthor.com

CPSIA information can be obtained
at www.ICGtesting.com
Printed in the USA
LVHW092038061120
670968LV00007B/1141